For Ella
and Teddy
I.W.

For
Joshua
K.P.

First published 2006 by Macmillan Children's Books
This edition published 2006 by Macmillan Children's Books
a division of Macmillan Publishers Limited
20 New Wharf Road, London N1 9RR
Basingstoke and Oxford
Associated companies throughout the world
www.panmacmillan.com

ISBN: 978-0-333-98218-1

Text copyright © Ian Whybrow 2006
Illustrations copyright © Kate Pankhurst 2006

The right of Ian Whybrow and Kate Pankhurst to be identified as the
author and illustrator of this work has been asserted by them
in accordance with the Copyright Designs and Patents Act 1988.

3 5 7 9 8 6 4 2

A CIP catalogue record for this book is available from the British Library.

Printed in Hong Kong

Ian Whybrow

Who's a Cheeky Baby?

Illustrated by
Kate Pankhurst

igloo

This cheeky baby
was playing with the keys.
He wouldn't give them back
when his mum said, "Please."

He held them very tightly
and he rattled them about.
His dad said, "Hey, Baby,
we're locked out!"

Along came the cat,
just as hungry as could be.
The cat said,

"Miaow!
I want my tea!"

The dog said, "Woof!
I'm hungrier than you.
Wait your turn –
I'm first in the queue!"

The cat said,

"Hissss!
I beg
your
pardon?"

The dog said,

"Grrr!"
and chased him
round the garden.

Mum said, "Quick dear, close that gate!"

The boy on the bike
gave a jiggle and a jump.

The man up the ladder said,

"Oh my gosh!"

He dropped his pot of paint
and the paint went . . .

The lady from the pet shop
got splashes on her dress.

The pets got a shock
and they all began to leap . . .

WHIZZ!

THUMP!

SPLASH!

YAP!

MEW!

FLAP!

CHEEP!

"SQUAWK!"
said the parrot,
as the animals went mad.

The baby laughed and
dropped the keys . . .

right in the
parrot's beak!

The parrot gave them back to Dad,
and kissed him on the cheek.

Then everybody smiled and said,
"Isn't that sweet!"
The pets settled down
and the parrot got a treat.

the dog, the cat, the boy on the bike,
the man up the ladder, the pet-shop lady,

the parrot, the mum, the dad and the cheeky baby all went back to the baby's house . . .